KARA AND FRIENDS MEET ABRAHAM LINCOLN

BY CAROLINE BREWER

AUTHOR:	Caroline Brewer
ILLUSTRATIONS:	Fort Wayne Area School Children
CONTRIBUTORS:	George Eldridge, Jr.
	Robin Robinson
LAYOUT:	H. Donald Kroitzsh

Copyright ©2003 by Caroline Brewer. All rights reserved. No part of this publication may be reproduced, stored in a retrieval system or transmitted, in any form, or by any means, electronic, mechanical, recorded, photocopied, or otherwise, without the prior written permission of the copyright owner, except by a reviewer who may quote brief passages in a review.

Printed in the United States of America

Published by:
Unchained Spirit Enterprises
PO Box 13143
Fort Wayne, Indiana 46867-3143 USA
Telephone: 260-458-0151
email: caroline@karafindssunshine.com
Website: www.karafindssunshine.com

Prepared by:
Five Corners Press
Plymouth, Vermont 05056 USA

KARA AND FRIENDS MEET ABRAHAM LINCOLN
ISBN: 0-9717790-4-X $17.⁹⁵

THE ILLUSTRATORS

Zack Archer	St. Jude School	1st Grade
Rachel Bougher	St. Jude School	3rd Grade
Liam Burke	St. Jude School	1st Grade
Jasmine Caldwell	Oak View Elementary	1st Grade
Leah Colley	Bunche Elementary	5th Grade
Kristina Dammeyer	St. Jude School	3rd Grade
Aaron Downham	St. Jude School	1st Grade
Alison Foldesi	Oak View Elementary	2nd Grade
Kathryn Manalo	St. Vincent de Paul	3rd Grade
Zachary Melchi	St. Jude School	3rd Grade
Ariana Nikolaenko	Weisser Park School	4th Grade
William Norfleet	Abbett Elementary	2nd Grade
Sloane Odle	St. Jude School	3rd Grade
Jason Robinson	Washington Ctr Elementary	5th Grade
Christay Smith	Bunche Elementary	5th Grade
Fantasia Smith	Abbett Elementary	2nd Grade
P.J. Sylla	Haley Elementary	2nd Grade
Simone Sylla	Haley Elementary	4th Grade
Bryan Tippman	St. Charles Borromeo	2nd Grade

Caroline Brewer's first book, **Kara Finds Sunshine on a Rainy Day** is available from:

Unchained Spirit Enterprises
PO Box 13143
Fort Wayne, Indiana 46867-3143 USA
Telephone: 260-458-0151
email: caroline@karafindssunshine.com
Website: www.karafindssunshine.com

ABOUT THE AUTHOR

If there's one thing you should know about Caroline Brewer, it's that she takes risks, loves to laugh, is irrepressibly optimistic, giving, loving, and almost too darn passionate about everything she does. Okay, so that's more than one thing.

Here's more. In the summer of 2001, Caroline threw away her old, comfortable life as an award-winning, Pulitzer Prize-nominated newspaper columnist in exchange for becoming founder and CEO of Unchained Spirit Enterprises, a motivational and educational publishing and seminar company.

Unchained Spirit also gives life to Caroline's books. Her first, which was partly inspired by the tragic events of 9/11/2001, is *Kara Finds Sunshine on a Rainy Day*. Entirely illustrated by elementary school children, this book of hope sold more 10,000 copies by December 2003 and was shared with more than 70,000 children and adults across the U.S., and in Bermuda, Haiti, England, Japan, and Papua New Guinea.

Kara and Friends Meet Abraham Lincoln is Caroline's second book. Many more are in the works.

DEDICATIONS

This book is dedicated to faith, friends, and family. For without these precious jewels of life, this book would not have been born.

Faith, as you will recall, is the EVIDENCE of things NOT SEEN. For the year that it took to take this book from conception to reality, there were times when I did NOT SEE how it would happen. But as the days and months went by, my faith increased. I knew the book would be real. I just didn't know how, and that's what makes life so beautiful and exciting.

My friends, who inhabit every region of the United States, and other parts of the globe, also made this book possible. My New Jersey and New York-based friends supplied unbelievably generous support to "Kara Finds Sunshine on a Rainy Day." The rousing success of that first book made this second one possible.

Old and new friends in Fort Wayne, plus many loving family members, picked up where my East Coast "family" left off. They include my mother, Ethel Brewer, sisters Liz Howard and Diane Brewer, brother Glenn Brewer, Uncle Frank, Uncle George, Aunt Sue, Aunt Juanita, Uncle A.C., Aunt Annie Bryant, nephew Marcus Brewer, and friends Vince and Robin Robinson, Camilla Kearnes-Grant, Alfred Curry, Wilhenda Jones, Asantewaa Daniels, Linda Michael, Harriet Miller, Rev. Gregory Guice and the Unity Christ Church of Fort Wayne.

This book is also dedicated to inspirational teachers, such as Ed Agresta of Wayne, NJ, who was the first teacher I ever heard call his students seeds.

ABOUT THE BOOK

In December 2002, a unique all-Fort Wayne collaboration began that led to the publication of this 40-page, 6-chapter children's book about Abraham Lincoln. The Everybody Reads Literacy Program contacted me and asked if I could write a children's story about Abraham Lincoln, an inspirational historical figure with strong Indiana roots.

Jane Wutrich was the enthusiastic and visionary program coordinator for Everybody Reads at the time. She worked closely with Steve Cebalt of Bottom Line Marketing. The pair became familiar with my work through my long-time friend, Vince Robinson, publisher of Fort Wayne's INK Newspaper. My most sincere appreciation to this wonderful trio for their vision and support.

I excitedly agreed to write the story. It is set in the third-grade classroom of a fictional teacher (based on a real-life teacher friend, Angeline Hall-Watts), and seeks to explore Lincoln's humanity.

One new chapter appeared weekly in the Journal-Gazette (where I first worked as an editorial writer) as part of the Newspaper in Education series, beginning February 12, 2003. More than 9,000 children throughout Fort Wayne and Allen County read the story.

All students were invited to submit illustrations for this book. Some 110 illustrations came in. I chose the best, and invited those children to workshops over the summer to give their art the three-dimensional effect needed for the book. Local Artist Robin Robinson (Vince's wife, and an expert in collage art) worked long, hard, and ever so patiently with the students to perfect their artwork.

The students were outstanding. Many worked for six hours over two days. None complained. They behaved maturely, intelligently, and allowed their creativity to shine. They made doing the book pure joy. My deepest appreciation to them, their parents and teachers.

On Oct. 14, 2003, 19 children from 8 Fort Wayne area schools were announced as winners in the illustration contest at a news conference with Mayor Graham Richard's Office. The contest and book were sponsored soley by me and Unchained Spirit Enterprises, and this is the beautiful result.

Many thanks to George Eldridge, Jr., my cousin, a talented and dedicated graphic designer, who helped this book become reality. Many thanks to his understanding wife, Phyllis, and daughters, Lavraea, Laniece, and Lanita for lending him to the project for so many long days and nights.

Warm thanks also to the Lincoln Museum in Fort Wayne which provided research support for the story and kindly offered to host the launch party for this book.

CHAPTER 1
THE PERRY BERRY SCHOOL PROJECT

It was top of the morning in January. The air was crisp and cool. Third-graders were seated at their desks at the Perry Berry Elementary School.

Rows were hung of bubble-gum-colored coats, mittens and hats. Students got ready to study the day's menu of important facts.

Children loved the Perry Berry School, because teachers taught in a way that was hot fudge sundae cool.

In Room 222, students never groaned about their teacher had them do.

For every assignment Ms. Angeline gave out, they couldn't help themselves but to shout a happy shout.

"Good morning, my seeds!" Ms. Angeline would cheerfully sing each day. "Good morning, Ms. Angeline!" the children would snappily, happily say.

Ms. Angeline called them seeds because her job was to help them grow. The children liked being called seeds. And they liked to be in the know.

In their hearts, Ms. Angeline held a special place. She was the best teacher, they believed, out of the entire human race.

"In a few weeks, my seeds," Ms. Angeline said, "we're going to have a special guest." Visions of this mystery person made the seeds hope Ms. Angeline would quickly tell the rest.

Ms. Angeline didn't make them wait. "February 12," she continued, "is our special date.

It's the day Abraham Lincoln, our 16th president, was born. This year, he'll visit on February 12, the very first thing in the morn."

A gasp sped across the room. It flew faster than the wicked witch on a broom.

Then, the most curious girl of all, Kara Contrera, stood up straight and tall.

Welcome
to Perry
Berry
School

She protested to Ms. Angeline, waving her hand like crazy. By the time Ms. Angeline responded, her 8-year-old mind had gone a little hazy.

"Ms. Angeline," she blurted out, "How in the world can that be? How can President Lincoln come to our school for us to see?

How can he possibly visit this room? Hasn't he been dead for a long time? Dead as the stick of a broom!"

All of Kara's classmates gleefully let go of their gasps. Then they filled up their school with the wildest bunch of laughs.

The children were not alone. Ms. Angeline got in on it, too. She chuckled in spite of herself. What else could she do?

For a minute it seemed the children's laughs would not be contained. Soon, though, they simmered down and let Ms. Angeline explain.

"Yes, you're right, Kara, our 16th president has been dead since 1865. But in many ways, my dear seeds, his spirit is still alive.

Although his body has passed away, much of what he did is still with us today.

"Abraham Lincoln lives on in museums and parks and statues and books. From these places, we can find out how he lived, including the favorite foods his wife cooked.

"So, when Mr. Lincoln visits our school in a few weeks, what you see of him will come from what you seek.

"You are going to bring Mr. Lincoln back to life. Tell what made him special. Tell of his successes and his strife.

"I want you to search high and low for Mr. Lincoln. I will give you the tools. We'll make it fun. And we'll definitely make it cool.

We'll never forget the special day that we brought Lincoln to life in our own Perry Berry way."

The seeds oohed and they aaahed, and their eyes shined like lights. They imagined having loads of fun, while working hard on their project each night.

Ms. Angeline next pulled out logs made of popsicle sticks. She stirred them in a box to make sure they were all mixed.

They looked liked those used to build the cabins Mr. Lincoln grew up in. One by one, she wrote down pieces of his amazing life on them.

"His library," said one log. "His homes," said another. "His family," another read, "and don't forget sisters and brothers."

"His kitchen," another log said, adding that children should tell about the kinds of foods he was fed.

Other logs listed parts of his body, such as his head, heart and chest." "Find out everything about Lincoln," the teacher urged. "I know you'll do your best."

With that, Ms. Angeline called up her seeds one by unique little one. Children took a log that put them on a team until every single log was gone.

Then she pulled out soft brown paper that slowly unrolled. It resembled the old-fashioned and ancient scrolls.

It was filled with all the places the seeds could do their digging, like the Internet, museums, and books. She sent them on their way to find what they could by hook or by crook.

When the school day was over, the seeds quickly dispersed. They dashed all the way home to begin their research.

CHAPTER 2
OH, THE PLACES WE WILL GO TO FIND MR. LINCOLN

Once Kara got home, she bounced up and down, twirled in circles, and flounced herself around. She couldn't relax. She couldn't be still. Joy ran through her like being on a ferris wheel.

Then, finally, her chance came to spill the beans. Her Uncle George and Aunt Sue arrived on the scene.

They were home at last. She had to spit out the good news of today. Spit it out fast.

"Uncle George!" she screamed. "Aunt Sue! Guess what amazing thing I've been given to do?"

Before either aunt or uncle could shed a coat, Kara let her thrilling news unload.

"On February 12, we will have a special guest, "the little girl said, nearly out of breath.

"President Abraham Lincoln is coming to our class. Even though he died, the good he did still lasts. We're going to bring him back to life by finding out about his past."

"That's very good news, little Kara," her Aunt Sue agreed. "Yes, dear," added Uncle George, "This will certainly help you grow as a seed. You can count on us to help you get all the materials you'll need."

"Thank you, Aunt Sue and Uncle George!" Kara Contrera exclaimed. "I'm going to treat this like an adventure, a treasure hunt, or a game."

After dinner, Kara, her aunt and uncle sat at the table mapping out a plan. They figured out how they'd bring back to life Mr. Lincoln, the president, and the man.

Kara told them that her classmates were split into teams of five to look into different parts of Lincoln's life.

"Our group chose the logs with Mr. Lincoln's body parts. I drew the log that reads 'Abraham's awesome heart'."

Uncle George said he'd take Kara to the library to check out books of all sorts. They'd look into Lincoln's childhood and careers, including his work as a lawyer in the courts.

Aunt Sue would take Kara to the Lincoln Museum in the city of Fort Wayne. As the largest museum about Mr. Lincoln, it holds plenty to fill a child's brain.

They'd both take turns on the Internet, and check out the Lincoln family pets. They knew *picturehistory.com* lets visitors view Lincoln's photos and statues. You can travel around, see each one, and never have to put on your shoes.

◁ Kara and Friends Meet Abraham Lincoln ▷
Caroline Brewer

The next day, Kara and her Uncle George set out for the library's children's room. All the way there, happy Kara skipped and sang herself a little tune.

They asked a librarian for as much help as she could give. The job of Kara's class was a big one, they said, to make Mr. Lincoln live.

"Here are biographies of Mr. Lincoln," the librarian said, "books that tell about his life from beginning to end. Some include stories from his family members, and some include stories from his friends."

There are books with some parts made up, she said, like one of how Lincoln used his hat as an extra head.

There is a story about Lincoln and letters he received from a slave girl. It's a story based on both the true and imaginary worlds.

Kara piled up so many books, they nearly plopped onto the ground. Her uncle lent a helping hand to keep his niece from tumbling down.

They checked out *Abe Lincoln's Hat,* and *Honest Abe,* and *Where Lincoln Walked.* Kara was so thrilled, she could hardly manage to talk.

They added *Lincoln: A Photobiography*, and *Dear Mr. President: Letters from a Slave Girl.* By now, Kara's hands were full of Mr. Lincoln's incredible world.

Uncle George checked out *With Malice Toward None.* With that, the pair's library researching was all done.

Kara rushed home, closed her bedroom door, began reading her books one by one on the floor.

She kept a pen and a pad nearby, so she could also take notes .She jumped into reading so quickly, she forgot she was still wearing her coat.

The next day, Aunt Sue escorted Kara to the Lincoln Museum, where her eyes kept hopping all around. Pictures, letters, and clothing from the president were just a few of the things she found.

The librarian told them about a small newsletter, called Lincoln Lore. Issue No. 270 was dated June 11, 1934.

It had lots of information about how Mr. Lincoln looked. Kara hadn't come across anything like this in all of her library books.

It described his head, his hair, his eyes, and the shading of his skin. It even gave information about his nose, his mouth, and his chin. Kara was so surprised and delighted, she could only grin.

This was just the kind of material her team in school would need. She felt lucky to have it, indeed.

On a weekend at Kara's home, all of the students in her group came to meet. They told Kara their research adventures were a very special treat.

They shared what they had found in their search for Lincoln's life. "And not just his successes," they sang, "We're also telling about his struggles and strife."

Abe Lincoln's Hat

Honest Abe

Lincoln: A Photobiograpy

Where Lincoln Walked

Letters from a Slave Girl

http://www.thelincolnmuseum.org

CHAPTER 3
LINCOLN'S HOMES

February 12 came quick as the blink of an eye. Scores of Perry Berry kids hugged and kissed their families good-bye.

Soon enough the students in Ms. Angeline's class were sitting in their seats. Their minds were hungry to dive into this school day's yummy treat.

A visit from Mr. Lincoln. The time had come after all. They knew it would be exciting. They knew they'd have a ball.

Juan Mendez was a member of Group Number One.

To tell about all the homes Lincoln lived in was his task. "Are you ready Juan, my seed?" Ms. Angeline softly asked.

"I'm ready," a smiling Juan said, nodding with his feathery-haired head.

Juan moved carefully toward the front of the class. He carried gently a small brown house as if it were made of glass.

The boy with shiny brown eyes breathed deeply, and let out a little sigh. Facing a roomful of curious classmates, he wished silently that his presentation be great.

"This is the kind of house Abraham Lincoln was born in in 1809," Juan began. "He lived in log cabins until he was all grown up as a man. The house I'm showing you this morning is made of fake logs. I found branches and sticks near the St. Mary River, where I used to go check out frogs.

"I used silly putty to keep the whole thing together. In Lincoln's day, a good log cabin kept out bad weather."

Lincoln was born in Kentucky, Juan said, around a place called Knob Creek.

～ Kara and Friends Meet Abraham Lincoln ～
Caroline Brewer

But just before he turned eight, his father felt it was time to leave.

Kentucky, he said, wasn't so good. He moved his family near Pigeon Creek, Indiana, and built another cabin in the woods.

Juan then pulled out a plastic bag of dirt and held it in his fist. "The Lincolns' floors," he said, "were made of only this."

Next, he pulled out corn husks and a piece of furry cloth. "When Mr. Lincoln was born, this is what his bed was made of.

The cloth I have is from fake animal hair, but in Lincoln's day, bed covers were made from a real bear!"

"Oooooh," Juan's classmates gushed, all at the same time. "I wish that bearskin bed cover was mine," shouted one redheaded little girl. "That would be the coolest bed cover in the whole wide world."

Juan then went to the corner and with another house came back. He didn't have to use silly putty in this one to fill in the cracks.

It looked like Lincoln's home in Illinois. The place he lived after growing up as a boy.

It was made of popsicle sticks and had two floors. Five windows went across the top. The bottom row had four.

"This is the first and only house Mr. Lincoln ever owned," explained the child. "He saved a long time to buy it. He was very, very proud.

"He lived in this house with his wife and four sons. There was lots of space for everyone."

"In this big house, the Lincolns had parties all the time. Their last party was when he became the 16th president, and left Illinois behind."

Juan took one last sigh. His nerves were calm, and his spirits pretty high.

No longer queasy, he figured it would be easy to tell about Mr. Lincoln's house in Washington, D.C.

Everybody knew what the White House was like. That place where presidential families spend most of their days and nights.

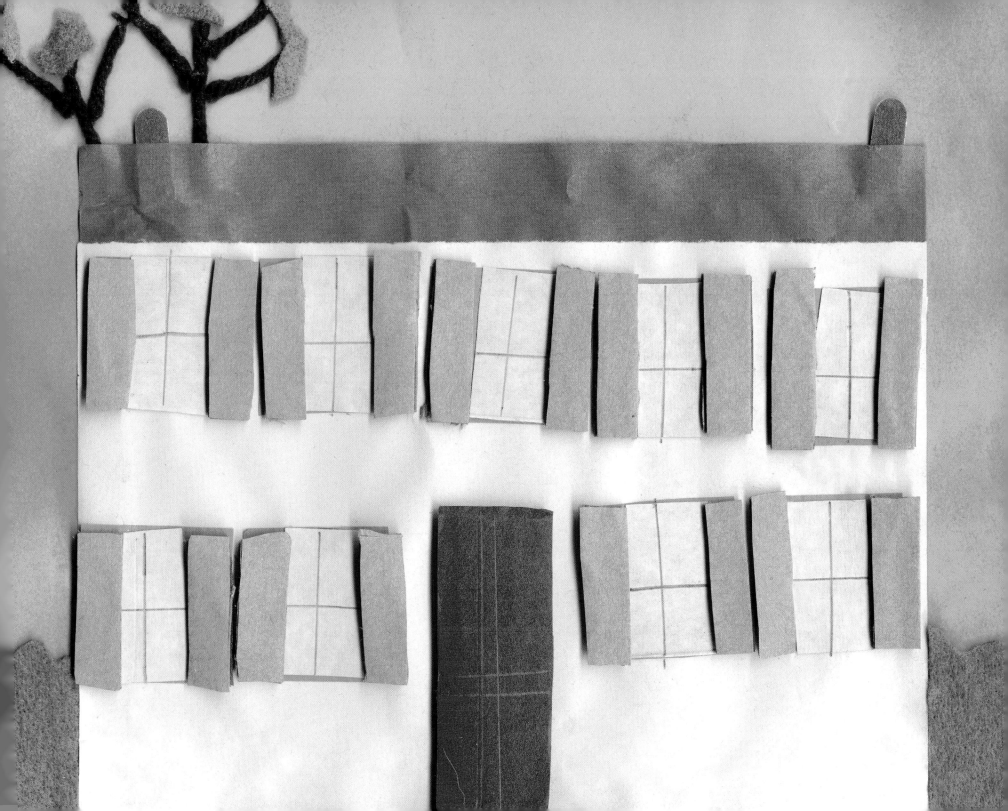

Juan held up a picture of the famous fancy house. "All the other presidents before only came with a spouse," he said.

"But this house was like a hotel. It had maids and cooks. And wall space for all of the president's books.

It had big closets to hang up lots of clothes and coats. It had room for Tad and Willie to keep big pets, like ponies and goats.

One goat slept in Tad Lincoln's bed. I think that might be a little too crowded," Juan laughingly said.

Juan folded up his project, smiled and took a bow. His classmates clapped their hands hard and they clapped their hands loud.

When the brown-eyed boy got to his seat, his heart was so happy, it nearly skipped a beat.

"Thank you so much, Juan," Ms. Angeline said with happiness. "You've done an excellent job, my seed. Your presentation was a smashing success."

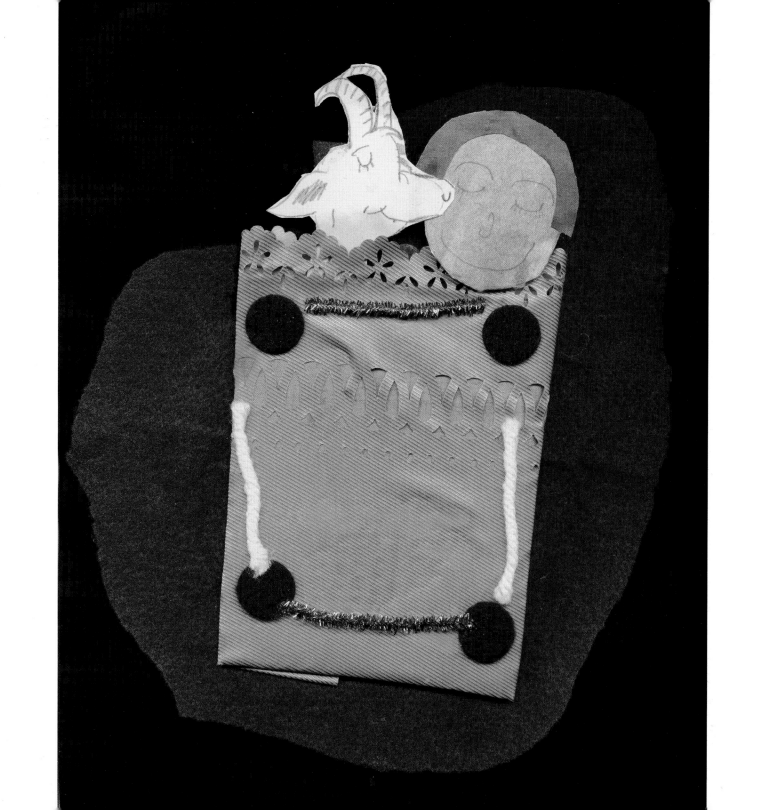

CHAPTER 4

MR. LINCOLN'S FAMILY

After Juan, it was Megan's turn. She was from Group Number Two. Telling her classmates about Lincoln's family was what she had to do.

Megan had hair that was sandy blond and eyes of ocean green. She was the perkiest little girl this Indiana school had ever seen.

She went to the front of the room, and from under a table pulled a box. She unloaded it with little toy people, whose clothes were made of socks.

She lined up the people across a table that was long and brown. She made some of them stand up and some of them sit down.

On the front of the table she set Thomas and Nancy Lincoln, Abraham's father and mother. To the side she set Abraham and sister Sarah. In the beginning, Lincoln had no brothers.

"Abraham and his sister, Sarah," Megan explained, "used to play in the fields together. They loved being outside, especially in warm, sunny weather.

They swam in the creek, and walked miles to get to a one-room school. Abraham loved his big sister. He thought she was really cool.

"Then one day, a sad thing happened in the family. Mr. Lincoln's mom, Nancy, got sick and she died. Abraham, his father, and Sarah spent a lot of time crying.

"A year later, Abraham's dad got a new wife. She already had three children and together the new family had a very nice life.

"Abraham's new mother was named Sarah, too. She decorated the Lincolns' old cabin; made it look like something new.

"When Abraham was 17, another sad thing happened in the family.

Sarah, his sister, moved away and got married. But when she was having a baby, she died. Abraham loved his big sister, and so again, for a very long time he cried.

"At age 21, Abraham moved to Illinois. He later married Mary Todd. They had four little boys.

Their names were Robert, Eddie, Willie, and Tad. Abraham loved to play with his sons. He was happy being a dad."

Megan pulled more people with clothing of socks from deep inside her cardboard box.

"In my hands is a toy doll of Mr. Lincoln's wife, Mary. She had long black hair in a bun and cheeks as rosy as a cherry," Megan told her classmates, who watched with wide eyes and listened with open ears. They paid her such attention, she moved ahead without fear.

"Mary liked dresses that were big and fluffy. She also put bands and flowers in her hair. Most of the times she took a picture," the child said, "she was sitting up straight in a chair."

Megan picked up a sheet to read. She had written down the rest for the seeds.

"There was a lot of love in Lincoln's family. But a lot of deaths, too, unfortunately.

First, Eddie died. He was almost four. Then, Willie died at age 11. Mary didn't think she could handle any more.

But Tad passed at 17. Mary thought life had treated her mean."

Still, when Mary was in the White House, she made one close friend. Elizabeth Keckly, a former slave, stood by Mary for years on end.

Elizabeth was at first hired to be a seamstress. For special occasions, she designed and sewed the First Lady's dresses.

They spent time together and made a special friendship grow. Elizabeth showed Mary that her gift was not just the fabrics she sewed.

Elizabeth's best gift was to lend her heart and hands to a friend. It helped the First Lady get through the tough times, over and over again.

When Megan first found out that so many in Lincoln's family had died, her 9-year-old heart felt crumpled inside.

To make herself feel better, she thought of a poem, and wrote down every letter.

It sounds like *Twinkle, Twinkle, Little Star*. The song children sing with their families in the car.

Twinkle, Twinkle Little Star, Bless Mr. Lincoln's family Wherever they are. Up above the clouds so high, Like angels resting in the sky. Twinkle, Twinkle Little Star, Bless Mr. Lincoln's family Wherever they are. Megan slowly, quietly walked back to her seat. The seeds applauded her project in a way that couldn't be beat.

Ms. Angeline patted her student on top of her head. "Perk up, little one," she smiled and said.

"You've shared what you could about Mr. Lincoln's life. Not just his successes, but also his struggles and his strife.

We know it was hard, but we're thankful, indeed. You did a great job, my precious little seed."

CHAPTER 5

MR. LINCOLN, ARMS AND LEGS

The seeds moved from chairs to a space on their knees. The next project team was Group Number Three.

They would build Lincoln's body. It wasn't close to small. It would stretch from the floor to the top of the wall.

Nyshon Green started off the show. His subject was Lincoln's legs and feet, but not his TOES!

Nyson had curly black hair and skin that was chocolate-brown. The child possessed so much confidence, you never caught him wearing a frown.

Nyshon took his spot in front of the seeds. His bag overflowed with the things he would need.

"Mr. Lincoln was tall and Mr. Lincoln was skinny. He stood six feet four inches, much taller than many," said Nyshon.

"Very few people in Lincoln's day could look him in the eyes if they had something to say.

He did not mind bending over to speak. He liked chatting with people. He thought it a treat."

Nyshon pulled out from his bag two legs mighty long. Black pants covered the cardboard; stood straight and strong.

"Mr. Lincoln used his legs and feet to do jobs that helped his family eat," said Nyshon.

"His legs helped him stand as he chopped trees for wood. They pushed a plow on the farm that grew all of their food.

As a man, his feet were a size 12 or 14. They were smaller, of course, before he was a teen.

His legs walked long miles with Sarah to school. Mr. Lincoln loved learning. No one could call him a fool."

Then Nyshon told of the time when Lincoln lived in Illinois. He was 19 and all grown up. No longer a boy.

He got a job as postmaster. He delivered the mail. Using his legs to travel, he did his job well.

Nyshon also told his class about the extra nice way Mr. Lincoln used those long legs one special day.

A lady paid too much for something from his store. So he walked several miles right straight to her door.

He gave her the change. She accepted with delight. "What an honest man," she thought, and "how very polite."

That's how Lincoln got the name Honest Abe. All that he owed, he made sure that he paid.

Nyshon then pulled out size 12 boots like the kind Lincoln wore. He'd found them on sale at the Goodwill store.

And that was just the start of presentations for Team Number Three. Jason Lambert was next up for the curious seeds.

Jason was a boy with light brown hair and round eyes. He didn't say much. Even his smile was shy.

But like all other seeds, Jason worked with zest. He quickly placed arms and hands next to the space for Lincoln's chest.

"Mr. Lincoln was a busy man. A lot of what he did, he did with his hands," Jason began.

"Before he grew real tall, he didn't play much at all.

At age 7, his father gave him an ax to chop wood. From the very beginning, this country boy's chopping skills were good.

The fast, fast way that Lincoln used that ax in his hands made one lady say he chopped like more than one man.

"Mr. Lincoln also used his hands to row a flatboat. One time it got stuck and it just would not float.

Lincoln's hands got busy to make the boat move again. Taking his time to solve the problem made him a smart man.

Mr. Lincoln liked using his hands to toss his sons into the air. He'd roll around on a rug with them, and mess up their dark brown hair.

Books were also something his hands LOVED to hold. Lincoln thought knowledge was worth a lot more than gold.

He didn't get to go to school for very long. Reading lots of books, though, made his mind super strong.

His hands kept happy, too, writing speeches and letters. He read and wrote for hours at a time, and got better and better.

Jason wrapped Lincoln's arms in a coat that was long. The president's body was taking shape. He looked tall and he looked strong.

The seeds cheered wildly for Jason and Nyshon. They represented their group well. They got the job done.

Chapter 6
Head, Heart, & Legacy

Samantha Moy walked swiftly and bounced into her place. The petite child with long black hair wore only happiness on her face.

Samantha had a job she wanted to do well. The ins and outs of Lincoln's head were what she had to tell.

She unloaded a cardboard face with a wig for Lincoln's hair. His black beard looked as fuzzy as a grizzly bear.

Samantha first told about Abe Lincoln's eyes. Dreamy and bright, they gave him special sight.

One man said his eyes were a soft gray, and had a way of looking far, far away.

Samantha said his eyes were like a crystal ball. He could see things that others couldn't see at all.

Before he became president, he gave the country a hint that slavery would end. Or else the North and South, he said, would never ever mend.

"Mr. Lincoln's ears and nose were a regular size," Samantha said to the seeds, looking them in the eyes.

"As a child, his ears often heard wild animals in the forests and the singing of birds.

His nose smelled the smell of hogs as they roamed the streets. It smelled foods like eggs and biscuits, some of his favorite things to eat.

"Mr. Lincoln's mouth did the most work. It talked for him to people who came to his country store. It told jokes and stories. It was never a bore.

 It won cases for him as a lawyer in the courts. It gave great speeches for elections, and occasions of all sorts.

"All that Mr. Lincoln did with his mouth usually started with his head," Samantha playfully said.

"When he was postmaster, and a lawyer, he would sometimes forget all the things he had to do. So he put notes and letters in his stovepipe hat. It was kind of a head No. 2.

His head was always busy thinking of things to write and say. One of his best speeches came to his mind came on a very sad day.

My mom helped me write a poem to explain it," Samantha told the seeds. She cleared her throat, stood up straight, and slowly began to read.

The Gettysburg Address was
about the war's greatest test
that great civil war battle
on a big giant hill
and the soldiers who fought there
with bravery and with skill.
They fought for the union

and the union they helped save.
In peace they now rest
in their Gettysburg graves.
Although Mr. Lincoln's speech
was just two minutes long,
the beauty of his words
is like the sweetest song.

The seeds were excited by Samantha's poetry. They applauded for what seemed like two minutes. Maybe it was three.

Kara Contrera would be last in the class to talk. Her long braided pigtails flopped around as she briskly walked.

Kara had to describe what went on in Lincoln's chest. She wished good luck to herself, and hoped for the best.

"The most important thing I can tell you about Mr. Lincoln's chest is that he had two hearts inside that held the secrets to his happiness."

Kara dug into her little bag of things, and pulled out two hearts tied with a golden string.

As the other seeds stared at Lincoln's hearts, their mouths dropped, and then formed a "Wow!" One of the hearts was split in two. "How could that happen?" they whispered. "How?"

"There are a lot of good reasons why one of Mr. Lincoln's hearts is broken in pieces," the child said.

"During the time that he lived, the American people were having a big fight. People in the South thought they had the RIGHT to treat black people really mean. Black people, they argued, were not like other human beings.

They thought black people were like toys or horses. Something they could sell and buy. They could sell a black mother's child. They could whip slaves until they died."

Kara swallowed hard as she thought more about what to say. She'd been planning for weeks to get everything right this day.

"Mr. Lincoln hated slavery. He thought all people should be free. But he also thought that people in the South were right when they said the Constitution gave them a GUARANTEE that they could keep slaves. They said they would fight about it to their graves.

All this talk of fighting and war was what made Mr. Lincoln's heart so sore. It's no wonder at all that it tore."

But then, Kara said, some of the things that made Lincoln's heart hurt and tear also made him feel warm and fuzzy as a teddy bear.

As she pointed to the heart that was full and round, her classmates kept quiet. No one made a sound.

Mr. Lincoln issued "The Emancipation Proclamation in 1863. It told the world that Southern blacks finally would be set free.

White and Blacks, including Frederick Douglass, called Lincoln brave. People danced in the streets. They came to the White House and waved.

Happily, snappily, they shouted his name. Lincoln cut the chains on America's greatest shame!

"Former slaves helped the North win the Civil War. When it was all over, Lincoln's heart was a lot less sore.

Moments like this filled Lincoln's heart with pride. He felt better about his presidency, and all who fought and died.

"And that's all I can say about Mr. Lincoln's two hearts. I put a golden string around them, so they will never part."

As Kara walked away to the tune of her classmates' cheers, the sweet sound of their applause was like music to her ears.

Ms. Angeline clapped long and loud for all the seeds in her class. "I'm so proud of the job you all did. You've created memories that will last.

"From Mr. Lincoln's life we can tell that he lived to treat others fairly. And he lived to treat them well.

He used his head, and his hands and his big giant heart to give America a new chance and freed blacks a new start.

He did the best with what he had. He did the best that he could do. That's the lesson of his life, my seeds, a lesson for you, and me, too."

**Graphic Design Consultant
George Eldridge, Jr.**

George Eldridge, Jr. is a graphic designer based in Fort Wayne, IN. He has lent his considerable talents to the design of fliers, brochures, business cards, letterhead and now a book. He will soon launch a clothing accessories line, featuring his own hand-drawn designs on 100 percent silk ties for men and scarves for women. He and his wife, Phyllis, have three lovely daughters.

**The Art Consultant
Robin Robinson**

Born and educated in Philadelphia, PA, Robin Robinson has created art in a variety of media and has provided art education and training to children and adults alike. Robin studied fine art at both Temple University and the Tyler School of Art. Her varied skills include drawing, painting, pottery, sculpture, doll making and photography. Currently, Robin lives in Fort Wayne, IN where she is the chief photographer for a weekly newspaper run by her family. She and her husband are raising three sons.